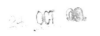

Also available:
Potions and Poison

Coming soon:
A Fighting Chance
Sword and Sorcery

For older readers:
The Dragon's Call
Valiant

Coming soon for older readers:
The Mark of Nimueh
The Poisoned Chalice

THE MAGIC BEGINS

Text by
Jacqueline Rayner

Based on the stories by
Julian Jones and Howard Overman

BANTAM BOOKS

MERLIN: THE MAGIC BEGINS
A BANTAM BOOK 978 0 553 82111 6

First published in Great Britain by Bantam,
an imprint of Random House Children's Books
A Random House Group Company

This edition published 2009

1 3 5 7 9 10 8 6 4 2

The Random House Group Limited supports the Forest Stewardship Council
(FSC), the leading international forest certification organization. All our titles that
are printed on Greenpeace-approved FSC-certified paper carry the FSC logo. Our
paper procurement policy can be found at www.rbooks.co.uk/environment.

Typeset in 16/22 Bembo Schlbk by Falcon Oast Graphic Art Ltd.

Bantam Books are published by Random House Children's Books,
61–63 Uxbridge Road, London W5 5SA

www.**kids**at**randomhouse**.co.uk
www.**rbooks**.co.uk

Addresses for companies within The Random House Group Limited can be found
at: www.randomhouse.co.uk/offices.htm

THE RANDOM HOUSE GROUP Limited Reg. No. 954009

A CIP catalogue record for this book is available from the British Library.

Printed in the UK by CPI Bookmarque, Croydon, CR0 4TD

With grateful thanks to
Johnny Capps, Julian Murphy,
Polly Buckle, Rachel Knight, Sarah Dollard,
Jamie Munro, Pindy O'Brien, Filiz Tosun,
Anna Nettle and Rebecca Morris

CONTENTS

CHAPTER ONE
CAMELOT!

Merlin reached the top of a hill and stopped. He'd been walking for hours and was tired, but he couldn't stop smiling – because finally the castle lay before him. Camelot! He stood and gazed down in wonder.

Merlin had hardly ever left the small village where he'd been born. He'd certainly never visited anywhere half as grand as Camelot, the amazing castle of King Uther that contained an entire city. It looked even more incredible than he'd imagined – the vast stone walls, the imposing battlements, the majestic turrets. And he was going to live there!

His mother, Hunith, had written a letter to the king's doctor, Gaius, asking him to look after her son. It wasn't that Merlin couldn't take care of himself – Hunith knew that he could. In fact, that was what worried her. The problem was, Merlin was . . . special.

Even Merlin didn't know quite how special he was. But someone – some*thing* – knew. A very old and powerful something that was waiting in Camelot for the boy to arrive. Before long, Merlin would meet the one who had been calling to him, and make some incredible discoveries about his own future.

But for now, never imagining what lay ahead of him, he shrugged his pack higher onto his shoulders, took a last look at the view behind him – where, if he squinted, he imagined he could still see the speck of Ealdor, his old village – and set off once more on his journey.

The hustle and bustle, the colours, the noise! Never had a place felt so alive. Nobody spared a glance for the dark-haired youth who stepped through the gates of Camelot many hours later, but Merlin didn't care. Why should they look at him when there was so much else to see? He laughed happily, the sound swallowed up in the hubbub of the city. Then suddenly, underneath the shouting and laughter and children's cries, he heard the *thump thump thump* of a drum.

Merlin pushed his way through the crowds, eager to see what was happening.

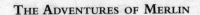

He was near the heart of the city now, the king's palace. Could that be . . . Yes! Coming out onto the balcony, the king himself, Uther Pendragon. But Merlin hadn't imagined that the lord of such a lively city would look so harsh.

He soon discovered the reason for the king's displeasure.

Guards dressed in chain mail led forward a peasant. The man's hands were tied behind him, and he looked exhausted and hopeless.

King Uther began to address the crowd. "Let this serve as a lesson to

AT THE CITY GATES . . .

all," he said. "This man, Thomas James Collins, is judged guilty of conspiring to use enchantments and magic. Such practices are banned, on penalty of death."

The man had been condemned to death – for using magic! The smile left Merlin's face. Suddenly his new life in Camelot no longer seemed like an exciting adventure. It was dangerous here.

Thomas Collins was led up onto a raised platform, where a man with an axe stood waiting for him. Merlin knew what was going to happen next.

He saw the king's arm come

down sharply, the signal for the axeman's arm to do the same, and he turned away. But he couldn't block out the swish of the blade – or the thud that followed it.

The sound had scarcely died away when Uther began speaking again. "When I came to this land, this kingdom was mired in chaos. But with the people's help, magic was driven from the realm. So I declare a festival – to celebrate twenty years since the Great Dragon was captured and Camelot freed from the evil of sorcery." The king was no longer stern. He smiled, inviting the people to join in the celebration.

But Merlin did not feel like celebrating – and he was not alone.

The crowd parted to let through an old woman. She lifted a tear-stained face to the king and cried: "There is only one evil in this land and it is not magic — it is *you*!"

"Mary, no!" came a voice from the crowd, but the woman was too upset to take any notice.

"You took my son, and I promise you — before these celebrations are over, you will share my tears." Her gaze flicked to the axeman's block before returning to Uther. "An eye for an eye, a tooth for a tooth — a son for a son!"

"Seize her!" cried the king. His guards ran forward as he shouted, but they were too late. Mary grabbed the pendant around her neck and muttered a spell.

The pendant glowed. Suddenly a whirlwind sprang up from nowhere. For a second it was impossible to tell where the woman ended and the tornado began, and then, in an instant, both were gone, leaving nothing but a few floating leaves as evidence of their presence.

Merlin looked back at the king. This was sorcery, and the boy could tell that Uther would make no allowances for a mother's grief. The woman had signed her own death warrant with her spell. That was what magic led to in this land. Merlin lowered his eyes quickly, suddenly anxious that the king might meet his gaze, pick him out of all the people in the crowd, realize what he was.

Worried and nervous, Merlin made his way through the crowd. He didn't think they'd seen the last of Mary Collins, and he wondered what exactly her threat meant.

CHAPTER TWO
MERLIN'S MAGIC

Merlin's fears dropped away as he entered the palace and concentrated on finding Gaius' chambers. As court physician, Gaius was responsible for the health not only of the king, but of all the people who lived in Camelot. Merlin wasn't sure if cleaning wounds and looking after sick people sounded all that much fun, but there were a lot of worse jobs – and it was an important position.

A sign directed him towards a door at the top of a narrow stone staircase. It stood slightly open, but he knocked anyway.

There was no answer. After a moment Merlin called out, "Hello?" Still nothing. He reached out a hand and pushed at the door. It swung open, revealing a large round room full of wonders: flasks full of bright, bubbling liquids, strangely shaped bottles, peculiar plants and more books than he'd ever seen in his life. Merlin stepped inside, dropping his pack by the door and gazing around. In one corner stood a pallet bed – perhaps Gaius slept as well as worked in here – and a twisting staircase led up to a high ledge which housed a collection of curious cabinets.

Rummaging through one of these was a silver-haired man, his back to Merlin.

The boy gave a small cough to attract the doctor's attention. Startled, Gaius swung

round – and lost his balance. There was a
dreadful splintering sound as the wooden
rail behind him gave way and a flash of
a terrified face . . .

And Merlin the nervous boy was no
longer there. In his place was Merlin the
warlock – for this was Merlin's secret; this
was what made him different from other
people. All his life he had been able to do
magic.

He could feel the magic building inside
him now, filling him with fire. The heat
rose behind his eyes, giving them a golden
glow. Everything slowed as the magic swept
through the chamber. Gaius now fell in
slow-motion, almost suspended in mid-air.

Merlin's gaze darted around the room
and spotted the pallet bed. Power flared up
within him again and a glance from his
golden eyes sent the straw-stuffed mattress
skidding across the floor to rest beneath

the plummeting physician. Then he released the magic and let everything return to normal. Time speeded up again – and Gaius made a soft landing.

Merlin wanted to cheer. He'd done it! He'd saved the doctor! But then he remembered Thomas Collins, who'd had his head cut off for sorcery, and realized how stupid it was to use magic in Camelot. He'd acted without thinking – he just couldn't allow a man to fall to his death. Merlin hoped that it had all happened too quickly for the doctor to realize what he'd done.

But Gaius hadn't been fooled. "What did you just do?" He was sitting up now, staring at Merlin. "Tell me! My bed wasn't here before, and you couldn't possibly have moved it in time!"

The boy took a deep breath. "It was nothing to do with me!"

Gaius was striding towards him now, and Merlin took a step backwards. "I want to know where you learned how to do it," the physician continued. "Where did you study magic?"

Merlin thought about running. But how far would he get before the guards caught him and forced his head onto the axeman's block, as they had Thomas Collins'? Then he noticed that Gaius didn't look angry, or shocked, or horrified – he looked astonished. So the boy made a big decision. His mother had told him that this man would look after him. That he was clever and wise. So he was going to trust him.

"I've – I've never studied magic. Or been taught. I was born like this," the young warlock stammered.

"That's impossible," Gaius snapped. "Who are you anyway?"

Merlin almost laughed. So much for his big revelation! But at least the doctor hadn't called the guards; hadn't had him arrested and dragged off in chains . . . "I'm Merlin," he said. "Hunith's son."

Gaius frowned. "Hunith's son? But you're not meant to be here till Wednesday."

Merlin wondered if it would be rude to point out to this wise man that it *was* Wednesday.

When the doctor realized that Merlin was who he said he was, he told him where to find the room that would be his from now on. Merlin picked up his pack and headed towards the staircase that Gaius indicated. There was still some tension in the air; each realized that he owed his life to the other, but knew it was better not to discuss it – at least not now.

But when Gaius called after him, "Merlin – thank you," the boy knew exactly what the old man was talking about.

The sight of his new quarters put a smile firmly back on Merlin's face. He had never had a room of his own before, and had never slept on a proper bed. He knew that to many in Camelot this sparsely furnished room would seem humble and mean but for him it was luxury. There were pillows and blankets! A cupboard! A table! And looking at it all, he suddenly realized he was no longer an ordinary village boy; no longer a child at his mother's side. He had his own place in the world now, and his new life stretched out in front of him, full of wonders.

He wandered over to the window and leaned on the sill. Blazing torches were scattered like stars across the city below, while hundreds of windows glowed with steady yellow candlelight. It was beautiful, and it was his world now. Spells and enchantments might not be allowed here – but still, at that moment the place seemed utterly magical, and Merlin was happy.

CHAPTER THREE

DOLL OF DEATH

Elsewhere in Camelot there was feasting. The nobles at court were happy to accept any excuse for a celebration, especially if the king had ordered them to be happy. But there was one person who was willing to stand up to Uther, and that was Morgana. She was a stunningly beautiful young woman with long

raven-black hair and dark eyes, but there was no look of admiration on Uther's face as he entered the moonlit chamber where she stood alone, gazing out of the window. "Why are you not joining us downstairs at the feast?" he demanded.

"I don't think that chopping someone's head off is cause for celebration," she said coolly.

The king frowned. "It is simple justice for what he did."

"He practised some magic! He hurt nobody," Morgana protested.

Uther shook his head. "You weren't around twenty years ago – you don't know what it was like. People must realize that there is no place for magic in my kingdom."

As he took his leave of her, Uther glanced back at the girl's face, set in stubborn disagreement. He didn't like arguing with Morgana – after all, she was his ward, the child he'd taken into his care when her father died. She was the daughter he'd never had – which meant it was even more important that she should be made to see his point of view.

Many miles from the city, Lady Helen of Mora was preparing herself for bed. She was a beautiful woman with long dark hair that she was brushing carefully; she was on her way to sing at King Uther's celebrations and he would expect her to look her best tomorrow.

A noise outside her tent made her stop for a moment. Was that a footstep? A twig cracking? She called out, "Hello?" There was no answer, and she started to get nervous. She called out again, this time for the captain of her guards, Gregory. To her huge relief, he appeared in the doorway, reassuring her that everything was all right.

But Gregory was wrong. Everything was far from all right.

Slipping magically past the guards came a figure carefully carrying a straw doll – but this was no child with a favourite toy. This was a wizened old woman with hatred in her heart. Mary Collins.

Lady Helen heard another twig crack

outside. She opened her mouth to call for Gregory again – but no sound came out. She tried to scream as the old woman thrust a dagger into the doll's body, but the pain in her own stomach was too great. Through some strange magic she was being made to suffer any injury that was inflicted on the doll! Mary Collins stabbed the puppet again and again, and Lady Helen fell lifeless to the ground.

The old woman smiled. The king had threatened her, showing nothing but contempt for an ugly crone. But he would react very differently to a lovely young woman – especially one who was his favourite singer.

Mary Collins muttered an incantation and her pendant began to glow, lighting up her haggard features – which slowly changed into the beautiful face of Lady

Helen of Mora. In the looking glass, her true visage could still be seen; the illusion was only in people's minds. But no matter, she would be careful. Because it was essential that she should be welcomed in Camelot with open arms – so that Uther Pendragon would come to know what it felt like to lose a son.

The next day, Merlin awoke with the strangest idea that someone was calling his name. But although he lay listening for a moment, all he could hear was the sound of Gaius moving around in the room below. He decided he must have been dreaming, and dragged himself out of bed. He didn't feel quite so excited about his new life in Camelot this morning – mainly because he wasn't quite awake yet. When he finally stumbled downstairs, the sight of the bowl of sloppy gruel that Gaius was setting out ready for him didn't really help.

The doctor glanced up as Merlin yawned his way over to the table. "There you are," he said, pointing to the gruel. "And I got you some water. You didn't wash last night." There was a full pail on the table. As the boy sat down, Gaius reached out a hand – and deliberately pushed the bucket.

"Merlin!" he cried urgently, and the young warlock swung round, saw the falling pail – and caught it.

But not with his hands — with his mind.

His eyes glowed with a golden light and the bucket stopped, its spilled contents hanging in the air like a frozen waterfall.

Merlin had acted without thinking — again. If there had been any doubts in Gaius' mind about the boy's magical abilities, they were gone now.

Panicking, Merlin quickly made the fire inside him die down. He released his hold on the bucket, and pail and water fell to the floor. His mind raced, wondering if King Uther had ways of detecting magic in his castle; if he'd found out about Merlin and had hidden men in the room, waiting to catch him out. But no sword-wielding guards jumped out of cupboards at him. There was just Gaius, staring at him in amazement.

"Tell me how you did that," the doctor said. "Did you say a spell in your mind?"

Merlin shook his head. How could he explain something that was as natural as breathing? "I don't know any spells. It just happens." He wasn't sure if Gaius believed him or not. It seemed like – well, like Gaius knew all about magic. Forbidden magic. But not about people who used it in the way Merlin did. Perhaps no one else used it that way? Could he really be the only one? Would that make Uther more lenient towards him if he found out – or much, much more ruthless? It didn't seem a good idea to discover which, and Gaius obviously thought the same.

"I'm not going to tell anyone," the doctor said. "But remember, the practising of *any* form of enchantment will get you killed. Do you understand?"

Merlin nodded. He understood all right. But he didn't know how he was going to hide it. Magic was a part of him, and he couldn't change that — even to save his life.

CHAPTER FOUR
A BAD START

Gaius had sent Merlin out to run errands, keeping him busy until he found a proper job – although what that might be Merlin wasn't sure. He wasn't afraid of hard work – back in Ealdor he'd had to help farm the land along with the rest of the villagers – but he didn't really fancy becoming a kitchen boy or a stable lad; not unless he could use magic to help out with all the boring bits, and that obviously wasn't a good idea.

Having delivered all the doctor's medicines, Merlin crossed the training yard on his way back to Gaius' chambers, and paused for a second to watch what was going on. A crowd of young knights were standing laughing as one of them, a tall, blond-haired lad, complained that a target was in the wrong place. His servant picked up the round wooden target and began to move it – as a dagger thudded into the circle's centre. The servant froze to the spot in alarm.

"Don't stop!" called the knight. "We want some moving target practice!"

Merlin watched with a frown as the boy scurried back and forth across the yard, the young knight throwing dagger after dagger at him – hitting the target spot-on every time. He would, of course. Merlin knew the type – even back in Ealdor there had been people like that, who thought that being good looking and skilful meant they could do whatever they liked. All the girls fancied them too. It was funny how girls couldn't spot how much of a prat someone was if that someone had big enough muscles.

Although . . . Merlin happened to glance up, and saw a girl who didn't look impressed. She was shaking a cloak out of an upstairs window, and there was definitely a frown on her face as she watched the blond lad laughing and joking with his mates.

Merlin was pleased to see that not everyone thought they were funny. He was getting more and more annoyed as he watched the poor servant weave his way across the yard. Suddenly the boy dropped the wooden target. He dived after it as it rolled away, and servant and target both landed at Merlin's feet.

"Hurry up, Morris!" called the knight, weighing another dagger in his hand.

But Merlin looked into the boy's anxious face and decided that things had gone far enough. He placed a foot on the target, preventing him from picking it up. "Come on, you've had your fun, my friend," he called to the young knight.

The lad raised his eyebrows incredulously. "Do I know you?" he asked.

Merlin held out a hand as the knight strolled across the yard towards him. "I'm Merlin."

The hand was ignored. "I don't know you – but you called me 'friend'."

Merlin looked into the arrogant face. He was suddenly aware that he had an audience; that a lot of people had stopped what they were doing to watch what was happening here. "That was my mistake," he said. "I'd never have a friend who was such an ass."

There were some laughs from the crowd. Merlin began to turn away, his job done. But the young knight hadn't finished with him. "Tell me, Merlin, do you know how to walk on your knees?"

Now it was the knight who was getting all the laughs, as Merlin said, "No."

"Well, I suggest you learn. Do you want me to help you?"

Merlin shook his head. This guy obviously wasn't used to people standing up to him and he didn't like it – but there was no way Merlin was going to kowtow to such a prat. Anyway, the knight didn't have a clue what he was facing. He might have that whole blond, strong, superior thing going on, but Merlin had magic! He smiled at the lad. "Oh, I wouldn't if I were you."

"Why, what are you going to do to me?" the knight said.

Merlin's smile grew wider. "You've no idea . . ."

The knight beckoned to Merlin, inviting him to throw a punch. A punch! As if Merlin needed to hit out with his hands when he had magic . . .

. . . magic that was forbidden, on pain

of death. In his head, Merlin again heard
the sound of the axe falling on Thomas
Collins' neck.

Hopelessly, he threw a punch. The knight,
taller, stronger and better at fighting,
grabbed Merlin's wrist and twisted it
behind his back. "I could have you thrown
in gaol for that," he said.

Still defiant, even through the pain in his arm, Merlin gasped out, "Who d'you think you are – the king?"

The lad grinned. "No, I'm Arthur – his son."

Merlin groaned as a pair of chain-mailed guards hurried forward and began to drag him off towards a castle cell. Of all the rotten luck! His first full day in Camelot, and he'd already made an enemy of the second most important man in the kingdom. Oh well. Surely things could only get better from here . . .

CHAPTER FIVE
GUINEVERE

Things could only get better – ha! A rotten tomato hit Merlin in the face and he shut his eyes hurriedly to stop the stinking juice getting in them. He'd thought things were looking up when Gaius came to see him in his cell that morning, to tell him he'd "pulled a few strings" to get him out – until Gaius mentioned that there was just one condition to this early release...And now here Merlin was, head and wrists locked in the stocks, trying to endure the barrage of old fruit and vegetables that was his punishment.

But he was thankful for one thing – it took his mind off the strange dreams he'd had during his night in the cell. Just like the night before, it had seemed to him that a voice had been calling his name – a deep, melodic voice that echoed right inside his head. But there had been no one there – no one even nearby. So it must surely have been a dream . . .

And here was another dream – it seemed like the barrage of rotten missiles had finally stopped. Could it be true?

Merlin opened his eyes. This time it was no dream. No fruit was flying towards him. Instead there was just a girl standing nearby. She looked familiar, and after a moment he realized where he'd seen her

before – this was the girl who had been watching Prince Arthur from a window and frowning. But now she was smiling shyly. "Hello," she said. "I'm Guinevere. But most people call me Gwen. I'm Lady Morgana's maid."

"I'm Merlin." Merlin put out a hand to her as best he could, still fastened into the stocks. "Although most people call me 'idiot'."

Gwen didn't laugh as she shook his hand; she looked concerned that he might really consider himself stupid. "No, I saw what you did – it was so brave. But of course you weren't going to beat Arthur."

Merlin tried to shake his head, although the stocks got in the way again. "Oh, I could beat him." Of course, he didn't tell her how. Or that it would probably result in his execution.

She seemed impressed, though, even as she questioned his answer. "You think? Because you don't look like one of those big muscly fellows, and Arthur's a real rough tough save-the-world kind of man ..." She trailed off as Merlin gave her an affronted look, then tried again: "No, I'm sure you're stronger than you look ... it's just ..."

"I'm in disguise," he said firmly, and she smiled again.

"Well, it was great you stood up to him. Arthur's a bully. And everyone thought you were a real hero."

Merlin grinned at her. He'd like to believe that. But a crowd of children were gathering near the stocks again, and he could see the bags of rotten fruit they carried. If that was how they treated their heroes, he'd hate to see what they did to their enemies. "Excuse me, Guinevere," he said. "My fans are waiting."

Later, Merlin sat down to eat with Gaius. This time the old doctor certainly didn't have to complain that Merlin hadn't washed: he'd scrubbed himself from head to foot to get rid of the smell of sour juice.

"D'you want some vegetables with that?" Gaius asked, indicating Merlin's plate with a knowing smile.

Merlin smiled back. But he knew that, behind the smile, Gaius was unhappy. "I know you're still angry with me," he said.

The physician sighed. "Your mother asked me to look after you. The one thing someone like you should do is keep your head down, and what do you do?" He shook his head. "What did your mother say to you about your gifts?"

Merlin shrugged. "That I was 'special'."

"You *are* special. The likes of which I've never seen before. Magic requires spells; it takes years of study. What I saw you do was elemental – instinctive. You do magic without even thinking about it."

Merlin thought again that Gaius seemed to know all about sorcery – even though it was supposed to be forbidden. Plucking up his courage, he asked, "Did you ever study magic?"

"Uther banned it twenty years ago,"

the old man insisted. But Merlin noticed that he hadn't actually answered the question . . . He didn't pursue the matter, though. He pushed away his plate, wondering if Gaius might instead be persuaded to explain some of the other things that had been puzzling him. Such as exactly why magic – that wonderful, useful, desirable thing – should be outlawed.

Gaius wrinkled his nose when Merlin put the question, but after a moment's thought he said, "Magic corrupts, Merlin. You're too young to know this, but people used magic for the wrong ends back then. It threw the natural order into chaos. Uther made it his mission to destroy everything from that time – even the Dragons."

The Dragons! Merlin had heard tales of them: huge flying beasts that breathed fire and could swallow a knight and his horse in a single gulp. But they were supposed to be magnificent to behold – and powerfully magical too.

"What, all of them – are they all gone?" he said, appalled.

Gaius nodded. "He feared them, you see. But there is one Dragon he chose not to kill, but to keep as an example. The Great Dragon. He imprisoned it in a cave deep within the castle – where no one can free it."

Merlin's mind was in a whirl. There was a Dragon – here! Here, in the castle, perhaps below his very feet! But he had no time to dwell on it. Gaius had changed the subject,

MAGIC CORRUPTS. UTHER MADE IT HIS MISSION TO DESTROY EVERYTHING, EVEN THE DRAGONS.

and was already listing his chores for the afternoon.

"Now, eat up. I need you to take this preparation to Lady Helen – she must have it for her voice."

"Lady Helen? Who's that?"

"Ah yes, you were . . . otherwise engaged when she arrived last night. Lady Helen of Mora – King Uther's favourite singer. She is to perform at tonight's celebrations." Gaius gave Merlin a pointed look. "Assuming she's been given that herbal mixture, of course."

Merlin took the hint. "Off to deliver it now," he said. But his thoughts weren't on some boring old singer. They were deep beneath the castle, flying with the Dragon.

CHAPTER SIX

RE-MATCH

Merlin had worried at first that he'd keep getting lost in Camelot's huge citadel, so much bigger than anywhere he was used to – but it hadn't taken him long to get his bearings, and there were always plenty of guards and servants around who were happy enough to point him in the right direction. So he found Lady Helen's chambers without too much difficulty, and knocked on the door.

There was no answer. Merlin waited

a few moments and then pushed the door open – just to check he really did have the right room. It seemed that he did. The clothes and trinkets scattered around the place were those of a noblewoman, anyway. He decided to leave Gaius' herbal mixture on the dressing table where it would be sure to be seen.

As he did so, though, he caught sight of something that seemed out of place – a small, crudely made, straw doll. A mascot, perhaps? Curious, Merlin reached out for it, and as he did so, he spotted the edge of a book, just peeking out from under a discarded scarf. He brushed the scarf aside to see the book better – and what a strange volume it looked! Merlin traced a finger over the runes on the cover, and was just about to open it when he heard a noise outside

the room. Someone was coming in!

Merlin hastily dropped the book back onto the table, and tried to look as though he'd not been anywhere near it. The newcomer was a beautiful dark-haired woman – but her lovely face was harsh and menacing as she stared at Merlin. "What are you doing here?" she demanded.

Merlin was already halfway out of the room as he answered. "I was asked to deliver your medicine," he said, hurrying out through the door without looking back.

But if he had turned his head, he

might have caught a glimpse of Lady Helen's reflection in the mirror – and he might have wondered why the glass showed the old, vengeful face of Mary Collins.

Merlin was so busy thinking about the strange book in Lady Helen's room that he didn't notice Arthur until he was nearly on top of him. The prince – surrounded, as he always seemed to be, by a group of admiring knights – was walking towards Merlin. There was nowhere to escape to.

Merlin tried to hide his face and just keep on walking past, but found a row of young men blocking his path.

"How's your knee-walking coming along?" asked the prince with a grin.

Merlin didn't answer. He attempted to edge round the knights, keeping his face turned away. *Keep out of trouble*, he was telling himself. *Just keep out of trouble* . . .

"Ah, don't run away!" Arthur called mockingly after him.

All Merlin's good intentions fled. "What, from you?" he sneered.

"Oh good, I thought you were deaf as well as dumb."

Merlin had a smile on his face as he finally turned to face the prince – but it was a dangerous smile. "I've told you you're an ass – I just didn't know you were a royal one. What are you going to do – get your daddy's men to protect you?"

"I could take you apart with one blow," boasted Arthur.

"I could take you apart with less than that."

They were looking at each other, both smiling, both dangerous. It was inevitable that they would fight. Before Merlin really knew what was happening, he was standing in front of the prince of Camelot, grasping a flail – a nasty-looking weapon consisting of a spiked ball attached to a handle by a chain.

Arthur had a flail too, and was handling it like an expert. He grinned. "I warn you, I've been trained to kill since birth."

Merlin realized that he couldn't fight like this. Without magic, the only weapons he had at his disposal were words. He faced up to Arthur. "Wow – and how long have you been training to be a prat?"

The prince shook his head astonished. "You can't talk to me like that."

"Sorry – how long have you been training to be a prat, *my lord*?" Merlin knew his only hope was to keep using those words – get the prince riled, force him to make mistakes—

Or, he thought as he crashed to the floor beneath Arthur's blows, *get him so irritated he'll swat me like an annoying fly. And here comes the final swipe . . .*

How Merlin loathed Arthur. How he longed to see him squirm. How he wanted the crowd to be jeering at the prince instead. He wanted it so much . . . that it happened. The familiar fire rose inside his body, turning his eyes amber. In their golden light, Arthur's flail became entangled in some tools that were suddenly hanging above him; he tripped on a box that appeared in his path, stumbled over a strangely taut rope, dropped his weapon – and there he was, at Merlin's feet. All at once it was the warlock who was in a position to deliver the winning blow. "Do you want to give up?" he asked.

The prince looked incredulous. "To you?"

Merlin gave him a victorious grin. But it dropped from his face as he saw who was watching him over Arthur's shoulder. Gaius was in the crowd – and he looked furious. Merlin realized with a jolt that he'd got completely carried away: his pride had made him risk his life just to wipe the smug smile off Arthur's face.

He was almost relieved to see that that smile was back on the prince's face as he took advantage of Merlin's distraction to knock him to the floor. This time, Merlin didn't try a thing. There was no question that Arthur was the victor. But as the guards rushed forward to drag Merlin to the cells again, the prince spoke. "He may be an idiot, but he's a brave one." He put out a hand and pulled Merlin to his feet. "There's something about you, Merlin . . . but I can't quite put my finger on it."

And as Merlin hurried off back to Gaius' rooms, unsure whether he'd just been very lucky or very *un*lucky, he hoped that Arthur wouldn't spend too much time working out just what was different about Camelot's latest resident.

CHAPTER SEVEN
THE GREAT DRAGON

It was obvious that Gaius was dying to shout at Merlin, but he restrained himself until they were safely out of earshot of anyone else. Once in his chambers, though, he exploded. "How could you be so foolish! Magic must be studied, mastered – and used for good, not for idiotic pranks!"

"He needed to be taught a lesson!" Merlin knew that the old doctor was right, and that made him belligerent. "Anyway, what is there to master? I could do magic before I could talk."

Gaius wasn't impressed by that argument. "Then by now you should be able to control yourself."

"I don't want to!" Merlin's genuine anguish shone through. "If I can't use magic, what have I got? I'm just a nobody, and always will be." He imagined the years stretched out in front of him, years spent as a kitchen boy or stable lad, doing hopeless, thankless tasks, being kicked around by the Arthurs of the world, achieving nothing. "Why was I born like this? I'm not a monster, am I?"

Gaius seemed horrified. "Don't ever think that."

"Then why *am* I like this?" Merlin cried. "Please. I need to know. Why?"

But Gaius — Gaius, who knew so much — had no answer to give him.

★

That evening, King Uther was dining with Lady Helen of Mora – or so he thought.

He was alone with the beautiful singer when the conversation turned to Arthur. "Will everyone be there tomorrow? How about your son?" she asked. "It seems a shame not to have met him."

Uther sighed. "That's Arthur for you!"

"Poor child, it can't have been easy to grow up without a mother."

The loss of his wife, Ygraine, was not a subject that Uther wished to dwell on and his face hardened, but the woman continued regardless. "That bond between mother and son is so hard to replace."

For a second the king was caught up in the grief that, for twenty years, had accompanied him – so he failed to notice

the hatred that appeared momentarily on his guest's lovely face.

While Uther dined, Merlin was dreaming of the deep voice again.

Long after the king and his guest had retired to their chambers, the dreams continued, and the young warlock twitched restlessly in his bed. And then he awoke – and the voice came again. It pulsed inside his head, and this time he was sure: it was real. It was calling him.

He jumped out of bed and made his way to the nearest corridor, being very careful not to disturb Gaius, who was asleep in the chamber below. Somehow he knew just where to go – he could detect the voice's presence, feel where it had come from. As he crept down towards the palace dungeons, he heard the voice again: "Merlin! Merlin!" it breathed.

There were two guards sitting by the entrance to the cells, playing a game of dice. Merlin had to get them out of the way – an easy job for a warlock. Suddenly the men found the dice bouncing off the table, heading for a far corner. The guards ran after the dice, but mysteriously they kept rolling just out of reach. Distracted by their chase, neither guard noticed a slim shadow slip by.

And then, after scrambling down what seemed like hundreds of stone steps, Merlin was suddenly in a cavern deep below the castle. He stood on a small stone ledge, staring out into endless darkness. He had been called here, he knew. But why? And by whom?

"Where are you?" Merlin shouted into the darkness.

"I'm here." The sound startled him, coming out of the gloom – but it was the same voice that had been calling his name, the voice he'd heard in his dreams. "How small you are!" it said now. Merlin fearfully stepped forward above the abyss as the voice continued: "For such a great destiny."

And he could suddenly see who had been calling him. There in front of him was the creature he had half expected to meet – the one who had haunted him ever since Gaius had spoken of it. A Dragon. More than that – *the* Dragon. The only one of its kind. The Great Dragon.

But what did it mean? "What destiny?" he asked.

The Dragon raised its great scaled head and stared him straight in the eye. "Your gift, Merlin, was given to you for a reason."

And suddenly Merlin felt that all his life had been leading him here, to this cavern, for these answers. The answers he so desperately needed.

"Arthur is the once and future king who

will unite the land of Albion. But he faces many threats, from friend and foe alike," the Dragon said.

Hang on, Merlin thought. *This doesn't sound like* my *destiny, it sounds like Arthur's!* "I don't see what that has to do with me," he replied.

"Everything. Without you, Arthur will never succeed. Without you, there will be no Albion."

HOW SMALL YOU ARE, FOR SUCH A GREAT DESTINY.

This has to be wrong, Merlin told himself. *There's no way I'm going to help that pompous, smug prat to rule the world!* "If anyone wants to kill him they can go ahead," he said. "In fact, I'll give them a hand."

The Dragon seemed amused by his reaction. "None of us can choose our destiny, Merlin – and none of us can escape it."

The massive creature suddenly launched itself into the air. Merlin was shocked to see the vast metal bracelet that encircled one scaly hind leg, with a chain attached that anchored the Dragon to the rocks. The links seemed stretched almost to breaking point as the Dragon flew up to a high ledge, far above Merlin's head.

"Wait!" the boy called in despair. "I need to know more!"

But his words fell hopelessly into the darkness, and there was no reply.

CHAPTER EIGHT

AN ENCHANTED EVENING

Merlin decided to say nothing to Gaius of his nocturnal adventures. The physician had slept through all his comings and goings, and seemed to accept the boy's bleary eyes and yawns as a normal state of affairs. He'd just asked Merlin to get up so that he could deliver a herbal potion to Morgana, who was suffering from nightmares.

Merlin was quite pleased to be given the task, despite having to drag himself out of bed. He'd heard about the beauty of the king's ward, and was interested in getting a glimpse of her for himself.

As it turned out, he almost got rather more than a glimpse . . .

There was no answer when he knocked on Morgana's door, and he reflected that no one in Camelot ever seemed to be in their rooms. But, as he let himself in and made his way to the inner chamber to leave

the potion for her, he discovered that he was mistaken. Morgana *was* there: she was behind a screen, getting changed. Merlin could see her elegant silhouette and had to fight to drag his eyes from it so he could get out of there. But as he turned to leave, Morgana started to speak.

Merlin froze. She must have heard him come in, and obviously thought he was someone else – she wouldn't chat to an unknown servant boy like this. What would happen if she discovered him there? His night in the cell would be a picnic compared to the punishment handed out for spying on the king's ward. And she was actually confiding in him – or whoever she thought he was – about her feelings

for Prince Arthur! How she didn't care a bit about him, how she resented being expected to accompany him to the feast that night. "If he wants me to go with him, then he should invite me, and he hasn't . . . so it means I'm going by myself," she said. "Pass me that dress, will you, Gwen?"

Merlin looked around for the dress. He had no choice but to play along until he could make his escape.

"Where are you?" Morgana asked impatiently.

"Here!" he tried in a high-pitched voice, holding the dress up in front of himself as she glanced over the top of the screen. To his amazement, the appalling impersonation seemed to pass muster. But how long could he keep this up?

"Gwen?" Morgana said again.

"I'm here," came another voice.

It was the real Gwen, the girl who had spoken to him in the stocks! Merlin had never been so pleased to see anyone. She smiled in amusement as he hurriedly passed her the dress and ran out of the room as fast as he could. That had been a lot more scary than facing a Dragon!

The great banquet that Uther had planned required a lot of servants, and Gaius had arranged for Merlin to be one of them. The boy didn't mind. He enjoyed just looking at the great hall with its rich wall coverings and vast hanging chandeliers, at the beautifully carved wooden tables laden with more food than he'd ever seen in his life before. This one feast would feed Merlin's entire village for a year – but he was in too good a mood to begrudge the guests their meal.

His mood improved even further when the Lady Morgana entered the room. Almost every eye in the room turned to her. "God have mercy!" Prince Arthur whispered as his jaw went slack. Morgana was wearing a dress that Merlin recognized, but he hadn't been prepared for the sight of her in it.

"She looks great, doesn't she?" said a voice at his elbow. He barely turned to acknowledge Gwen standing beside him. "Some people are just born to be queen."

Merlin was horrified. This vision of beauty was going to marry that prat Arthur? "No!" he said.

"I hope so. One day. Not that I'd want to be her – who'd want to marry Arthur?" Gwen continued, and Merlin could only nod in agreement.

He was forced to tear his eyes away

from Morgana as the nobles made their way to their places at the tables. She was sitting to one side of Uther at the top table, with Arthur on his father's other side. Merlin found himself stationed just behind the prince. He only hoped Arthur wouldn't notice him and send him on some humiliating errand; he wouldn't put it past him. But for now, Arthur's attention was politely fixed on the lady in the centre of the room, as his father stood to introduce her.

"We have enjoyed twenty years of peace and prosperity," the king announced. "It has brought the kingdom and myself many pleasures. But few can compare with the honour of introducing Lady Helen of Mora."

The audience applauded as the beautiful woman composed herself to sing. She grasped a pendant at her neck as if

it were a good-luck charm.

The first sweet notes echoed round the hall, and Merlin smiled. How great it was to be here, to be part of this amazing place, to be hearing such wonderful singing . . .

But Merlin was magical, and magic spoke to him. Something was not right here. This was no ordinary song, no ordinary voice. He stuffed his fingers in his ears, trying to block out the siren sounds.

All around him, courtiers were collapsing as the voice wove its spell. Cobwebs grew over their sleeping forms as food rotted on their plates in front of them. Only Merlin stood awake and aware as the singer moved down the hall towards the top table – towards the king and his son. Yes, Merlin was pretty sure it was Arthur she was watching – but why?

As she drew a dagger from her sleeve and raised it high, he had the answer. She was going to throw it at Arthur – she wanted to kill him! And suddenly the things he'd said to the Great Dragon

about letting anyone kill Arthur were just words. He could never stand back and watch someone be murdered – and, he realized, he didn't hate Arthur, not really.

The golden fire rose in his eyes. Up above the singer, the chain holding the giant chandelier snapped. The great metal wheel crashed down, pinning the woman to the ground. The knife clattered to the floor. The song died. And the court began to wake.

CHAPTER NINE
DESTINY CALLS

The courtiers brushed cobwebs from their faces and stared in astonishment at the figure on the floor. The last thing they remembered was a beautiful singer standing in front of them; now suddenly there was an ugly old crone lying beneath a fallen chandelier. Uther and Arthur both stood up, moving forward to see better.

Merlin too was amazed at the transformation, but suddenly everything made sense. He recognized the old

woman – it was Mary Collins. "A son for a son," she had said to the king, and this had been her attempt at revenge. She had disguised herself with magic, and her anger and sorrow had brought her here – to try to kill Uther's child as he had killed hers. Merlin couldn't have let Arthur be murdered, but part of him found it hard to blame the grief-stricken Mary Collins for her actions.

In front of them, the old woman raised her head. The hatred in her eyes as she stared at father and son was intense. And there before her was the fallen dagger. With a last gasp of effort, she reached out – and suddenly the blade was

flying through the air towards Arthur's heart.

No one could save him. Still dazed from the enchanted sleep, no one was thinking clearly, no one could move quickly enough.

No one except Merlin. The heat soared through his body. His eyes flashed with gold, and the world slowed down. The dagger spun lazily across the room, turning in sluggish circles as Merlin dived towards the prince – grabbed his shoulder – and pulled him down.

The blade thudded into the back of Arthur's chair, the fire in Merlin's eyes died, and time speeded up again.

Mary Collins lived just long enough to see her plan fail. Arthur lived, and the king would continue to slaughter magic-users without a second thought. As the courtiers began to cheer, the grieving mother took her final breath and lay still.

Suddenly it was Merlin who felt as though he were in a magical daze. He was surrounded by cheering, applauding people – and one of them was the king himself. Uther looked somehow more alive than Merlin had ever seen him before as he grasped Arthur's shoulder, smiling with joy. He didn't – he couldn't – suspect that Merlin had used magic; he was just happy to have his son still.

"You have saved my boy's life," he said to Merlin. "You shall be rewarded!"

Merlin tried to look modest, but he was

bursting with excitement inside. Comfort! Riches! The Lady Morgana's hand in marriage!

"This merits something quite special," said the king. "You shall be awarded a position in the royal household. You shall be Prince Arthur's manservant."

The whole room cheered – except Merlin and Arthur. They looked at each other in disbelief. *This* was a reward?

Merlin escaped from the feast as soon as possible and fled to his own room. People seemed to want to *congratulate* him on becoming Prince Arthur's new servant! Did they really think that being at the beck and call of that big-headed idiot was a *good* thing? He just hoped Arthur wouldn't try to throw daggers at him, like he'd done with his last servant — Merlin would find it very difficult not to resort to magic then. But, perhaps the king wouldn't even notice if Merlin turned Arthur into a frog — after all, the prince was already quite slimy.

Merlin looked up in alarm as the door opened, but it was only Gaius. The old man carried a bundle under his arm, which he placed on the table.

"Seems you're a hero," he said with a smile.

Merlin smiled too. "Hard to believe, isn't it?"

"No. I knew it from the moment I met you. You saved my life, remember?"

Merlin shrugged. "But that was magic."

"Yes." Gaius nodded. "And now it seems we've finally found a use for it. You saved Arthur's life — perhaps that's its purpose . . ."

"My *destiny*?" The Dragon's words soared into Merlin's mind. The reason for his magic, his gift. Could it be true after all?

Gaius pushed the cloth-wrapped bundle towards him. "This book was given to me when I was your age. But I've a feeling it will be of more use to you than it was to me."

Merlin carefully lifted the cloth. There lay a large leather-bound book with silver clasps. He clicked them open. Inside . . .

"But this is a book of magic!" Page after page of spells, of charms and enchantments, pictures of flowers and herbs and magical beasts . . .

"Yes. Which is why you must keep it hidden," Gaius told him solemnly.

Merlin grinned. A book like this – he would guard it with his life! "I will study every word," he told the good, kind man in front of him – a man who, he suddenly realized, must have many secrets of his own.

He opened his mouth to ask a question – but a shout came from outside. "Merlin! Prince Arthur wants you right away!"

Gaius looked amused. "Your destiny's calling," he said. "You'd better find out what he wants."

And putting the precious book carefully to one side, Merlin jumped to his feet – and ran off towards his future.

CHAPTER TEN

THE SINISTER SHIELD

Destiny! Merlin cursed the word as the man whom he was supposed to protect hit him over the head with a sword. The *clang* as the blade bounced off his helmet echoed in his ears for at least half a minute. Merlin waved his own sword around, hoping he might block some of Arthur's blows by luck, because he certainly wouldn't manage it any other way. This painful and one-sided combat was the prince's idea of practising for the tournament that would begin the next day. Merlin wasn't really sure how hitting someone who barely knew which end of a sword was which would help Arthur when it came to fighting proper knights, but the prince was now his master and he had to obey his commands, however silly they might be. In the short time he'd been Arthur's manservant he'd had to wash the prince's socks, muck out his horses and clean his boots after a dog had been sick on them, but today's activities really took the biscuit. And what made it even worse was that the prince really seemed to enjoy heaping this humiliation on him.

Merlin was still grumpy when he staggered into Gaius' chambers that evening and collapsed into a chair. He was exhausted and sore, but he couldn't even go to bed because he had to learn all about tournament etiquette and armour by the next morning. He pointed to a huge book lying on the other side of the table and it shot magically towards him, its pages turning of their own accord to the entry on armour.

Gaius was not amused. "What have I told you about using magic like that?"

"If I could actually feel my arms, I'd pick up the book myself." Merlin winced, remembering all the blows Arthur had landed on him, seemingly with great enjoyment.

"Never mind your arms – what am I going to do if you get caught?"

Merlin looked at the old man. He'd not thought about that before. What *would* Gaius do?

The doctor simply shook his head

when Merlin posed the question. "You just make sure it doesn't happen — for both our sakes."

Merlin grinned at him. As if he'd be so foolish as to use magic in public after all he'd been through recently!

But if the boy had known what was happening at a market just a few dozen miles from Camelot at that very moment — if he'd had any idea what the next few days would bring — that smile would have been wiped from his face.

Knight Valiant made his way through the booths, searching for one particular stallholder. This was no ordinary market — there were no sellers of vegetables or cooking pots or cloth. The goods these stalls offered would earn their owners execution if King Uther ever learned of their existence. But Valiant showed no nerves: he had the confidence of the born fighter who feared no one. He was a man in his thirties, dark, ruggedly good-looking — and very ambitious.

He reached his goal and ducked inside a tent. The stallholder, Devlin, greeted him eagerly, anticipating the gold that would soon be coming his way.

"I understand you have a shield for me," Valiant said.

Devlin nodded, pulling aside a blanket to reveal his illicit wares. The shield bore an unusual design: three snarling snakes with fangs bared.

Valiant smiled at the sight of it. "Show me how it works," he demanded.

The stallholder began to chant a series of seemingly meaningless words — but they formed a powerful enchantment.

Three living snakes dived out of the image on the shield and hissed menacingly at the knight, who jumped back, surprised.

"When you're competing in the tournament, you pin your opponent under the shield" – Devlin mimed the action – "and a snake strikes. Your opponent will be paralysed in seconds." He handed the shield to Valiant, saying, "The snakes are now under your command – they will do anything you tell them to do."

Valiant smiled, bowing his head to look at the snakes. "Kill him!"

He left the tent a few minutes later, very satisfied with his new shield. He looked around warily, but if anyone had heard the scream of the stallholder, they'd decided not to act – this market was a place where people minded their

own business. Valiant wove his way through the stalls, retrieved his horse, and rode off towards Camelot.

CHAPTER ELEVEN
PREPARING TO FIGHT

Inside a small house in Camelot, Merlin was feeling extremely foolish. Yesterday he'd merely hated being Arthur's servant; today he thought that it would be more fun to swap jobs with the boy who cleaned out the castle privies. At the moment Merlin was wearing full tournament armour – not an outfit he would have donned through choice. But hours of study overnight hadn't made much impression on him, and he needed to know how to put it all together before the tournament began in a couple of hours' time. Gaius had suggested enlisting the help of Gwen – as the daughter of a blacksmith she was used to armour, and Merlin, remembering how kind she'd been to him before, thought it was worth a try.

So now he was apparently dressed in voiders, hauberks, gauntlets, greaves and all sorts of other metal bits and pieces that seemed more like instruments of torture than a protective covering.

Gwen smiled sweetly at him. "It suits you. You look like a knight."

Merlin tried to believe her, but couldn't quite manage it. He could see his face reflected in a breastplate, and was quite sure that no knight would look quite so wide-eyed or panic-stricken.

He took a deep breath. Trumpets were sounding in the arena – the tournament was about to begin. He had to get over there and face Arthur. That is, if he could get this armour off again . . .

With a lot of help from Gwen – Merlin couldn't believe how difficult it was to undo buckles when you were in plate mail – he made it to the tournament ground just in time, and began to dress Arthur in his armour. Somehow, though, it seemed almost impossible to copy exactly what Gwen had shown him only a short time before. Arthur's armour was a lot more complicated than the suit he'd practised with, and it was hard to tell which way round all the pieces went.

"You do know the tournament starts *today*?" Arthur commented as Merlin struggled with a wrist guard.

"Yes, sire. I'm aware of that." He stepped back, hoping he'd finally managed it.

Yes, it seemed that most bits of Arthur had metal over them, anyway. Well, except his head – and Merlin certainly wouldn't want to see anyone swinging a sword into Arthur's unprotected skull, oh no. Abandoning a brief, happy vision, he thrust a helmet into the prince's hands and stood back to admire his work. "Great. I think you're all set."

Arthur didn't move – just stared at his servant. "Aren't you forgetting something . . . ?"

Merlin looked at him blankly. He'd done it all, he knew he had. Every single bit of armour was now on Arthur's body somewhere.

"My sword!"

Whoops. Merlin gave Arthur what he hoped was a winning smile. Of course he hadn't forgotten his sword – it was just a little joke . . .

He wasn't fooling anyone, and Arthur did not look amused. "Oh yes, you'll be needing that," said Merlin as he handed it over.

Arthur just snatched the sword and strode off. Merlin gazed after him in dismay. He was trying so hard – but it was all going wrong. If he couldn't even kit out Arthur for a simple tournament, how was he supposed to help him become the once and future king? The land of Albion was doomed before it had even been created.

A giant scoreboard stood at the end of the tournament

ground. The name and colours of each knight made a long line at the bottom of the board. The Pendragons' gold dragon was there, alongside the colours of each of Camelot's knights, as well as those of the various visiting fighters.

After each bout, the colours of the losing knight would be cast from the display, while the victor's crest would be raised to the next level. As the rounds of the tournament went on, more and more badges would fall, until only two were left. Those who had won through would then face each other in the most fiercely fought contest of all – to become tournament champion, winner of a thousand gold pieces and the privilege of escorting the Lady Morgana to the victory feast.

There wasn't an empty seat anywhere. Every noble in Camelot had come to watch the fighting, and many others had travelled far to be there. Inside the nearby castle, all the servants had left their work and had their noses pressed to the windows, hoping to see some of the action. As Merlin came into the tournament grounds, ready to stand on the sidelines in case the prince wished to order him around some more, he actually felt grateful for a moment that he was Arthur's servant – at least it meant he got a good view.

An excited hubbub rose from the stands as the knights filed into the arena. They wore cloaks in rich colours – purples, reds, golds – and each had his personal crest embroidered on his tunic. As they came to a halt in the centre of the arena, a trumpet fanfare sounded. The crowd hushed, and King Uther rose to address the assembled knights.

"Knights of the realm – it is a great honour to welcome you to Camelot. Over the next four days you will put your bravery to the test . . . and your skills as warriors. And of course, you will challenge the reigning champion – my son, Prince Arthur."

Reigning champion. Merlin hadn't known that, although he should probably have guessed. He ran his eye along the row of knights, hoping to spot one who might give his royal highness a run for his money, and hopefully a sore head too. And there was a man who seemed to fit the bill. A knight maybe a dozen years older than Arthur, dark and arrogant, looking intently at the prince as if summing him up as an opponent. The man had a distinctive shield bearing a motif of three striking snakes, and Merlin thought it might be a good idea to keep an eye on him.

Uther was reaching the end of his speech. "It is in combat that we learn a knight's true nature, whether he is indeed a warrior — or a coward." He paused for a moment, letting the words sink in, then turned to the crowd. "Let the tournament begin!"

The knights headed out of the arena.

Only the two who were to fight first remained. A young knight called Alfred – and the reigning champion, Arthur. Attendants removed their cloaks and strapped their shields to their arms. And then the fighting began.

CHAPTER TWELVE

THE TOURNAMENT BEGINS

It was soon clear to Merlin why Arthur was the reigning tournament champion. He wasn't just strong, he was skilful too; it was more like watching a dance than a fight. The knight Alfred was quickly dealt with. Pellinor and Kai soon followed. As Arthur dealt yet another winning blow, Merlin found himself cheering with the crowd. He hurriedly stopped himself — as if he *wanted* Arthur to win! The prince was quite big-headed enough as it was.

But when Arthur managed to parry a seemingly unstoppable sword swipe by Bedivere, Merlin yelled out, "Yes!" Again he hastily shut his mouth, looking from side to side to check no one had spotted his enthusiasm. But it was difficult to hide it. Arthur the warrior was very different to Arthur the prat who ordered him about. The prince's bravery was matched only by his gallantry. He fought better than anyone Merlin had ever seen, but never pursued an unfair advantage. If his opponent tripped, he waited for him to get up. If Arthur knocked the other man's shield to the ground, he allowed him to pick it up again. Like everyone watching, Merlin just couldn't help but admire this bold, honourable knight.

By the time Bedivere crashed, defeated, to the ground, Merlin didn't even notice how loud he was cheering. His every grievance was forgotten, and Arthur was his hero.

Valiant too was moving up the rankings. His sword play wasn't as stylish as Arthur's, but it was effective. Several members of the crowd were overheard wondering whether Valiant's brawn would overcome Arthur's technique, but they weren't to find out that day as the two knights' names were never drawn against each other. As the first day of the tournament came to a close, there was much anticipation of even better entertainment on the morrow.

As Merlin removed Arthur's armour, Valiant himself came over to congratulate the prince on his victories. "Creep," said Merlin as the knight left, still caught up in his new role as Arthur's biggest fan, and

Arthur smiled his agreement. For a second they were friends.

But the moment passed and they were immediately master and servant again: and Arthur wasn't going to let a servant speak like that about a knight. Merlin was soon put in his place. "For tomorrow, you need to repair my shield, wash my tunic, clean my boots, sharpen my sword and polish my chain mail."

As the prince listed the numerous chores, Merlin reflected that life as Arthur's manservant meant never sleeping again. That is, unless he got some help . . .

"Merlin!"

The warlock looked up in alarm at the sound of Gaius' voice. In front of him, a hammer was beating out the dents in Arthur's armour, a stone was sharpening Arthur's sword and a cake of soap

was scrubbing Arthur's tunic — all by themselves. Merlin himself was sitting with his feet up, reading his precious book of magic.

"Are you using magic again?" Gaius demanded as he came in.

"No," said Merlin guiltily as the evidence crashed to the floor.

Gaius just shook his head in frustration.

Elsewhere in Camelot, the knights were lining up to be introduced to the city's nobles. Valiant bowed as he was greeted by Uther. "I am Knight Valiant of the Western Isles, my lord."

"I saw you fighting today. You have a very aggressive style," Uther replied.

Valiant nodded, taking this as a compliment. "As my lord said, to lose is to be disgraced."

The king was clearly impressed with Valiant – and he wasn't the only one. Standing next to Uther was Morgana, who smiled in pleasure as the knight moved along to greet her and kiss her hand.

"I understand the tournament champion has the honour of escorting my lady to the feast," Valiant commented.

Morgana nodded. "That's correct."

"Then I will give everything to win the tournament," he said.

I AM KNIGHT VALIANT, MY LORD.

Morgana was still smiling at Valiant as the next knight moved forward to meet her – Arthur. The prince was also watching Valiant, now chatting to a group of courtiers – but he wasn't smiling. Morgana noticed his scowl, and was amused. "They all seem rather impressed by Knight Valiant," she commented, hoping to rile him some more.

Arthur looked her straight in the eye. "They're not the only ones."

"What's the matter, Arthur?" said Morgana. "You're not jealous, are you?"

"I can't see there's anything to be jealous of," he replied sharply.

Morgana flushed at the insult. One all. She turned to Gwen, standing behind her, as the prince moved off. "Could Arthur be any more annoying? I do hope Knight Valiant wins the tournament."

Gwen looked uncertain. "You don't really mean that," she said.

"Yes, I do," Morgana insisted, not wanting to admit even to herself that Arthur could get under her skin so much.

CHAPTER THIRTEEN
SNAKES ALIVE!

Merlin rose bright and early and headed over to the armoury to prepare Arthur's equipment for the day's events. No one else was there when he arrived, and he thought pityingly of all the other knights' menservants, who were probably grabbing as much sleep as possible after a long night of chores.

Suddenly he heard a faint hissing sound. He turned ... No, he was still alone. He must have imagined it. But then the noise came again.

"Hello?" he called. There was no answer. But he'd definitely heard something. Merlin decided to investigate.

He crept through the rows of weapons and armour, following the sound. Rounding a corner, he prepared to confront the culprit – but there was no one there. All there was in front of him was Knight Valiant's shield with the three painted snakes.

But . . . No. Surely not. He had to be imagining it. Because for a moment he thought he saw one of the snakes blink!

Curiously, Merlin crouched down to examine the shield more closely. He reached out a hand to the image . . . and froze. The tip of a sword was just touching his chest.

He stood up slowly. Valiant was holding

his sword point straight at Merlin. "Can I help you with something, boy?" he growled.

Merlin tried to look as innocent as possible; tried not to let on that he had seen anything out of the ordinary – indeed, he still wasn't entirely sure that he had. "Nope, I'm good. I was just gathering my master's armour."

"Then you'd best be on your way."

Merlin couldn't have agreed more, especially as Valiant hadn't lowered his sword yet. He hurried away, gathered up Arthur's armour as quickly as he could, then didn't stop until he was back in the castle.

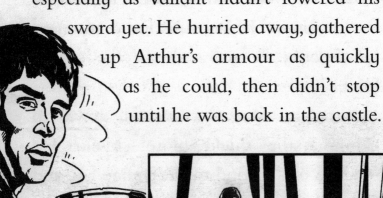

He might have been imagining the blinking snake, but he certainly hadn't imagined the knight's anger, and he felt a little scared. He'd have to try to steer clear of Knight Valiant in future.

He cheered up, though, a short time later, watching Arthur's reaction to his gleaming armour, his spotless clothes, his polished boots and his shiny sword. "You did all this on your own?" the prince asked in amazement.

"Yes, sire," said Merlin truthfully, waiting for a compliment to follow.

Arthur wasn't prepared to go quite that far yet. "Well, let's see if you can get me

into it without forgetting anything."

That wasn't a problem. With magic to do his jobs for him, Merlin had had plenty of time to get to grips with the finer points of kitting out a knight.

"That was much better," Arthur said as Merlin finished buckling the last strap, then handed over the prince's sword with a flourish. "Not that it could have got any worse," he added.

"I'm a fast learner," Merlin told him, accepting that this was as close to a compliment as Arthur would get. He didn't mind. There was something strangely satisfying about seeing the young knight walk out into the arena in his sparkling armour, knowing that they were – even in a rich/poor, master/servant, prince/dogsbody way – a team. Later on, he didn't even feel embarrassed when Gaius spotted him cheering for Arthur.

"Is it my imagination, Merlin, or are you beginning to enjoy yourself?" Gaius asked.

"Well, it isn't totally horrible all the time," the boy admitted.

The second day of the tournament continued much like the first. Arthur won all his fights – and so did Valiant. Again, neither was drawn against the other, so each continued his devastating rise up the rankings.

It wasn't until the afternoon that Valiant first found himself facing a serious challenger. Ewan was one of the knights of Camelot, and Arthur himself had taught him to fight. He expertly parried most of Valiant's best moves and landed a few good blows in return.

Valiant's face darkened as he saw victory slipping away – especially as he

was very aware of the Lady Morgana watching intently in the crowd. He would *not* be beaten!

Summoning up all his strength, he sliced at Ewan, sending him stumbling back towards the edge of the arena. Valiant followed through, slamming his shield into the winded man and pinning him to the ground. There, with his shield facing away from the crowd so no one watching would be able to see the snakes, the knight whispered: "Strike him!"

Ewan had no breath to cry out as a snake rose out of the shield's crest — he could only watch in horror for that brief

second before the serpent sank its fangs into his neck.

The crowd was applauding Valiant's victory as Merlin and Arthur looked on. "I think Ewan's badly hurt," Merlin whispered, noticing that the knight wasn't getting up. Then they saw Gaius hurrying into the arena and kneeling by Ewan's side.

Merlin frowned and Arthur nodded at him gravely. "Go with Gaius," he told him. "It looks like Ewan needs all the help he can get . . ."

As Merlin entered Gaius' chambers, he realized it was worse than they'd imagined. Ewan was unconscious, sweating and twisting on the bed.

"How is he?" Merlin asked.

"It's most odd . . ." the doctor replied, tailing off as he looked at his patient.

"But Valiant only knocked him out," protested Merlin.

Gaius beckoned him over. "Look at this," he said, pointing at the knight's neck. "Two small wounds. It looks like a snake bite. He seems to have been poisoned."

"But how can he have been bitten by a snake?" asked Merlin. And then he remembered that morning. He'd thought he'd seen a snake blinking on a shield, and if it could blink, why couldn't it do more – why couldn't it bite? And who had that shield belonged to? Knight Valiant, of course.

"I don't know . . ." Gaius began, but his voice trailed away. Merlin was no longer there.

★

Merlin crept down the palace corridor towards the visiting knights' chambers. If Valiant had a magic shield, he was going to find out about it. He thought of Arthur, so noble in battle – and then there was this evil knight, who might be using magic to cheat in the tournament; might actually be using it to try to kill people! Merlin had always thought magic was a good thing, but Gaius had explained how some people used it for the wrong ends. Obviously this was the sort of thing he'd meant. Well, Merlin wasn't going to let it happen.

He found Valiant's room, opened the door carefully, and peered inside. There weren't any snakes in sight – but to the boy's surprise there was a cage of mice. He hadn't pictured Valiant as an animal lover.

Just then the knight himself strode into view. Merlin ducked back, but it was all right – Valiant wasn't looking in his direction. Instead, he went to the cage and pulled out a mouse by its tail. Merlin inched a little further into the room so he could see better. There was the shield, propped up on a chair, its crest of entwined serpents clearly in view.

Valiant held the helpless mouse over the shield. "Dinner time!"

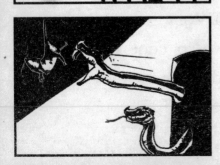

A snake darted out of the crest, mouth open wide. Merlin's eyes were just as wide as he watched the serpent devour its prey. He hadn't been imagining things that morning in the armoury. This was definitely an enchanted shield. And it was deadly.

CHAPTER FOURTEEN

AN ANTIDOTE

Merlin hurried back from Valiant's chambers to tell Gaius what he'd seen. But to his frustration, Gaius didn't seem to take him seriously. "Are you sure? Is there a chance you were mistaken?" he asked.

Merlin shook his head. "I know magic when I see it. Ewan was fighting Valiant when he collapsed. It must have been one of the snakes from the shield that bit him. I'll have to tell Arthur."

But Gaius didn't look happy. "Maybe there's another explanation. You can't go accusing a knight of using magic without proof. The king would never accept the word of a servant over that of a knight. And how would you explain why you were in Valiant's chambers?"

Merlin wanted to scream. "But—" he began.

Gaius held up a hand. "That's just the way it is," he said with finality.

Merlin still felt hurt and confused the next day. He knew what he had seen – and he knew that Gaius believed he had seen it. But for some reason the physician preferred to shut his eyes to Valiant's evil magic, even though he had the proof of its power in front of him: Ewan was still unconscious, and growing weaker by the hour.

The young warlock avoided Gaius as

best he could. He spent most of his time watching Valiant, hoping to pick up any clues, any signs that might convince others that magic was being used. But there was nothing. Even when Valiant delivered a killing blow to an opponent, Merlin could see no hint that magic had been involved.

He stared gloomily at the scoreboard as the dead knight's colours were discarded. The tiny shield clattered on top of a pile of others, representing the many fighters who had lost over the course of the day.

There were now only two emblems left on the scoreboard. One showed Valiant's entwined snakes; the other was the golden lion on a sable background that was the crest of the Pendragons. Tomorrow Valiant would fight Arthur, but all the prince's fighting skills would be no match for a deadly magical snake.

Gaius came over and joined Merlin. The

boy didn't look at him, still too angry about his words of the day before. Didn't the doctor realize how serious this was? "Valiant's going to fight Arthur in the final," Merlin told him, his face stony. "He'll use the shield to kill him." He finally turned and looked Gaius straight in the eye, waiting for the old man to pour out apologies for what he'd said earlier. But Gaius remained silent. Merlin shrugged his shoulders in disgust and walked away. He'd thought he'd found an ally when he came to Camelot – but Gaius wasn't willing to help him after all. Somehow, Merlin would have to work this out by himself.

He returned to Gaius' chambers, glad that the old doctor wasn't there. Poor Ewan still lay on his bed, looking even worse than he had before. As Merlin stared down at the dying knight, he knew that he couldn't let the same thing happen to Arthur.

The door opened and Gaius walked in. Merlin didn't even acknowledge him: he felt too angry. But the doctor came over and began to speak. "Look, Uther really wouldn't listen to you or me," he said. "But you were right. We can't let Valiant get away with this."

Merlin was pleased that Gaius had changed his mind. It was a relief not to feel so alone. But even so, it didn't really alter things. What Gaius had said yesterday was still true – they didn't have any proof that Valiant was using magic. But the doctor had come up with a plan: if Ewan recovered, he could tell the king himself. Uther would believe another knight.

It was a good idea, but it still didn't get them any further. Ewan was unconscious, and didn't seem likely to wake up. "If only we had an antidote," Gaius said. "But I'd need the venom of the snake that bit him to make one, and I—"

He turned round and stopped. Once again, Merlin had vanished.

Merlin crept up to Valiant's room for a second time. But he knew that King Uther was hosting a dinner for the tournament's finalists: this time Valiant would not be inside. The door was locked, but that was no hindrance to someone with Merlin's powers, and in a few seconds he was on the other side. There was the shield, propped up on a chair as before. Valiant's sword stood in a rack nearby, and Merlin helped himself to the blade. He didn't take his eyes off the serpent crest for a moment as he tiptoed up to the chair – he'd seen how quickly the snakes could move.

But suddenly Merlin heard a sound

from outside the room. Foot-steps? He turned to the door – just as a snake began to uncoil. It sprang from the

painted image and struck out angrily, fangs bared. Merlin spotted it just in time and hopped backwards in alarm. Then he remembered what he was there for. He chopped downwards with Valiant's sword – and there was the snake's head, lying at his feet. He snatched it up just as the serpent's two fellow snakes

leaped from the shield, then he sped out of the room, leaving the door open behind him.

Merlin was in such a hurry to get away that he didn't notice someone coming down a side corridor. Knight Valiant had returned from the feast – and he'd spotted the slight figure fleeing from his room.

Leaving Gaius to get started on an antidote using the extracted venom, Merlin went to find Arthur. Oh, he and the prince still weren't friends, Merlin knew that. They were too different, came from separate worlds. But something had happened over the course of the tournament – a kind of respect had grown between them. Merlin had seen a different side to Arthur, and perhaps the prince had sensed that too. He'd been more polite to his servant, less irritated. He might not actually go so far as to listen to what Merlin had to say – but that was going to have to change, because Merlin had a very important story to tell.

It wasn't easy to convince Arthur of the truth, even with the snake's head as proof – although the prince actually found it more difficult to believe that his incompetent servant had chopped the head off a magic snake than that such a snake might exist in the first place. "Ewan was pinned under Valiant's shield – no one could see the snake bite him," explained Merlin.

"But Valiant wouldn't dare use magic in Camelot," Arthur protested. "I don't like the guy, but that doesn't mean he's cheating."

Merlin held out the severed head. "Have you ever seen any snakes like this in

Camelot? Gaius is preparing an antidote to the venom. When Ewan's conscious, he'll tell you what happened." He looked straight at Arthur, willing the prince to believe him. "I know I'm just a servant. My word doesn't count for anything. But I wouldn't lie to you. If you fight Valiant in the final, he will use the shield to beat you."

Arthur held his gaze. "I want you to swear to me that what you're telling me is true."

"I swear it's true."

"Then I believe you."

Merlin grinned in relief. Arthur trusted him. Ewan would tell everyone what had happened, and Valiant would be stopped. No one would die.

Everything was going to be all right.

But what Merlin didn't know was that as Gaius administered the antidote to Ewan

CHAPTER FIFTEEN
TELLING THE TRUTH

The entire court of Camelot had been summoned. Arthur and Valiant stood before the king, watched by a host of knights and courtiers. Morgana was there with Gwen, both extremely curious to find out what Arthur had to say.

The prince did not leave them wondering for long. Without ceremony, he announced: "I believe Knight Valiant is using a magic shield to cheat in the tournament."

There were gasps from the crowd. Uther turned to Valiant. "What do you have to say to this?"

"My lord – this is ridiculous," the knight replied, sounding astonished. "I have never used magic. Does your son have any evidence to support this outrageous accusation?"

"I do," Arthur asserted. He gestured to Merlin, who held out the snake's head. The prince took it and gave it to his father, explaining what it was. Uther then asked to examine the shield. "Be careful, my lord," Arthur said as Valiant handed it over – but nothing happened. No snakes struck.

He can control them, Merlin thought. *He left them on guard in his room – that's why they attacked me there – but he's not going to risk them coming to life in front of the king.*

"It seems to be an ordinary shield,"

Uther said. "Do you have any witnesses to its magical properties?"

Arthur nodded. "Knight Ewan was bitten by one of the snakes from the shield. The venom made him grievously ill – however, he has received an antidote. He will confirm that Valiant is using magic."

"Then where is this witness?" demanded the king.

That was just what Merlin was wondering. Gaius had promised to bring Ewan along as soon as he was strong enough – they didn't want to annoy Uther by making him wait.

He breathed a sigh of relief when the door opened and Gaius came in. But the old doctor was on his own. Merlin hurried over to meet him. "Is Ewan all right? Did he tell you what happened?"

Gaius looked very solemn. "After I gave

Ewan the antidote, he told me everything. The snake on Valiant's shield came to life and bit him."

Merlin was very relieved. "That's brilliant!"

But Gaius shook his head. "He was still weak from the venom, so I went to prepare a strengthening potion for him. When I got back, he was dead – and there were more snake bites on his neck."

Merlin gasped in horror. "Oh no!" He hadn't really known Ewan, but he'd seemed nice. He certainly hadn't deserved to die like that. And – Merlin glanced back at the king, who was looking extremely impatient – their plan had died with him.

They had to keep going, but they had little chance of success now. Except... well, Uther knew that Merlin had once saved Arthur's life – maybe the king

would believe he was telling the truth,
even if he was only a servant. They had
to try.

He hurried back to Arthur. "Ewan's dead,"
he whispered.

The prince unhappily turned to tell Uther
the news. "I'm afraid the witness is dead.
But my servant fought the snakes from the
shield—"

The king cut him off. "You're making
wild accusations against a knight on the
word of your *servant*?"

Arthur took a deep breath. "I believe he's
telling the truth."

Merlin was amazed – and pleased. He'd
half expected Arthur to give up, not to
support him in the face of the king's obvious
displeasure.

Valiant had been listening to all this
with a look of injured innocence on his
face. Now he appeared indignant. "My

lord, am I really to be judged on some hearsay from a boy?"

"I'm not lying. I've seen the snakes come alive." Merlin knew as soon as he'd said it that it was a mistake. Uther had nothing but contempt for servants, even those who'd saved his son's life.

"How dare you interrupt! Guards! Take him to the dungeons."

Two Chain-mailed guards hurried forward to do the king's

bidding. But to Merlin's surprise, Valiant spoke. "My lord, I'm sure he was merely mistaken. I wouldn't want him punished on my account."

"You see," said Uther, directing his words at Arthur, "this is how a *true* knight behaves – with gallantry and honour."

Valiant smirked at Arthur's discomfort. "My lord, if your son made these accusations because he's afraid to fight me, then I'll graciously accept his withdrawal."

Oh brilliant, Merlin thought. *He comes across as all noble and understanding, impresses the king and humiliates Arthur at the same time. Could this go any more wrong?*

Merlin's last hope was that Arthur would insist on it being the truth. But he knew that couldn't happen now. Without proof, everyone would just think he was a coward, afraid to face Valiant. So he was unhappy but not surprised when Arthur backed down. "There's obviously been a misunderstanding," the prince said. "I withdraw the allegation against Knight Valiant." He turned to the knight, and Merlin caught the quick flash of satisfaction on the knight's face as he graciously accepted Arthur's apology.

Arthur turned and strode out of the room, his cheeks flushed with embarrassment. Merlin hurried after him. "I know that didn't go exactly to plan," he said, realizing that it was a bit of an understatement. "Look, we could break into Valiant's chambers and try to provoke the snakes—"

He stopped as the prince turned to stare at him with something like hatred in his eyes. "I believed you. I trusted you. You made me look like a complete fool. My father and the entire royal court think I'm a coward."

As he met Arthur's gaze, Merlin almost stumbled backwards in shock. The prince was trying to hide his pain, but it was so raw, so bitter, that for a moment Merlin almost felt it too. Suddenly he realized what it must be like to be Uther's son – to have to live up to the impossible standards of a harsh, cruel king who expected so much and gave so little. Merlin thought of his own loving, kind, sweet mother, and for the first time actually felt sorry for Arthur. Confronting Valiant in front of the king had required more bravery than facing him in battle, and yet everyone now thought the prince was a coward.

"We can still expose Valiant," Merlin said, desperate to help.

But Arthur turned away from him. "No," he said. "I no longer require your services. You're sacked. Get out of my sight!"

CHAPTER SIXTEEN

TWO HALVES OF A WHOLE

Merlin couldn't believe he'd been dismissed by Arthur. A few days ago he'd have given anything to get out of serving the prince – but over the course of the tournament he'd changed his mind. He'd begun to think that there might have been something in the Dragon's words: that Arthur was indeed destined to be a great king; that he, Merlin, was supposed to help him along the way.

But now he was convinced that the Dragon had been talking rubbish – and the sooner the creature realized that, the better.

Merlin made his way down to the deep cavern, but to his surprise the Dragon was nowhere to be seen. The boy had no intention of leaving without saying his piece, though. He shouted into the darkness: "I just came to tell you, whatever you think my destiny is, whatever it is you think I'm supposed to do – you've got the wrong person. That's it. Good-bye."

He paused for a moment, waiting, but there was no reply – just the faintest echoes of his own words bouncing off the rock. So he turned to leave – only to come face to face with the Great Dragon.

WHATEVER YOU THINK MY DESTINY IS, YOU'RE WRONG.

"If only it was so easy to escape one's destiny," said the beast.

"How can it be my destiny to protect someone who hates me?" Merlin asked.

"A half cannot truly hate that which makes it whole — very soon you shall learn that."

Great, thought Merlin. *Just what I need . . . another riddle.*

"This is not the end, young warlock," the Dragon continued. "It is the beginning." And with a flap of its leathery wings it was gone, leaving Merlin more confused than ever.

After his encounter with the Dragon, Merlin had wandered around the castle for a bit, pointlessly, unhappily, and had finally come to rest on a set of steps overlooking the main square, where he sat with a face as gloomy as those of the two stone dogs on either side of him.

He barely looked up as Gwen joined him. "Is it true what you said about Valiant using magic?" she asked.

He nodded.

"What are you going to do?" she said.

Merlin sighed. "Why does everyone seem to think it's down to me to do something about it?"

Gwen gave him a sad little smile. "Because it is, isn't it?"

And he had to accept that she was right. Whether or not he believed in this business of "destiny", he was the only person – apart from Gaius – who truly believed that Arthur's life was in danger. Unless the rest of the court saw Valiant's treachery for themselves, they'd never accept it.

That was it! Somehow he had to make the snakes come alive in front of everyone . . .

He stood up, full of purpose, and grasped hold of one of the stone dogs. With a determined heave he . . . totally failed to pick it up. "Er," he said, turning back to Gwen, "do you have a wheelbarrow . . . ?"

CHAPTER SEVENTEEN
A PRINCE'S DUTY

The sun went down as Merlin sat in his room with the stone dog, desperately trying to master the incantation that brought inanimate creatures to life. Somehow he had to make Valiant's magic visible so that everyone could see the snakes for themselves.

He went over and over the words in the spell book, practised the gestures it listed – but the statue remained still. Merlin kicked it in frustration, and hurt his foot.

This wasn't going to work. He wasn't used to casting spells like this – what he did was instinctive magic, not structured or disciplined.

Another hour passed. Merlin had barely moved, save to kick the statue again or pick up the spell book from where he'd thrown it across the room.

He had to face it. Sorcery wasn't going to save Arthur, not this time. He had nothing left to try but words – and they'd hardly helped so far. But what else could he do?

Merlin made his way to Arthur's chambers. The prince had only just removed his armour, having been practising as long as the light lasted. He wasn't pleased to see Merlin.

"I thought I told you to get out of my sight," Arthur snapped.

"Don't fight Valiant in the final

tomorrow. He'll use the shield against you."

Arthur didn't look at him. "I know."

"Then withdraw," Merlin said desperately. "You have to withdraw."

"Don't you understand? I can't withdraw. The people expect their prince to fight. How can I lead men into battle if they think I'm a coward?" The prince did look at him then, and Merlin suddenly understood that Arthur knew he was facing death – but saw no other choice.

"Valiant will kill you. If you fight, you die—" replied Merlin.

"Then I die. But I have to fight. It's my duty."

And for a prince – for Uther's son – it was as simple and terrible as that.

Merlin went back to his room, filled with a terrible dread. He had to keep

trying with the spell, it was Arthur's only hope. But at the moment it felt more like no hope at all.

Merlin wasn't the only one who had a bad night. The next morning Morgana woke from a terrible dream in which Arthur had been at Valiant's mercy. Somehow it had all felt so real, and she was troubled.

What if Valiant was using magic after all? Unknowingly echoing Merlin's thoughts, she wished that Arthur would withdraw from the contest. For once in his life, why couldn't he be a coward?

She rose from her bed and Gwen dressed her. Then she made her way to Arthur's chambers. She didn't try to talk him out of fighting – it would be no use; she'd known him long enough to be sure of that – but carefully and calmly she helped the prince to put on his armour, piece by piece, just being close to him, supporting him without words. They had been like brother and sister for years, since Uther had adopted Morgana after her father's death. Like many siblings, they bickered and fought a lot. But there was something else between them too, something unspoken and rarely shown that drew them together now.

As Arthur turned to leave, Morgana knew she had to say something – but the right words just weren't there. "Be careful," was all she managed, and Arthur acknowledged it with a small smile. She knew he would do his best, she knew he would fight as bravely and strongly and skilfully as ever – but she also knew it would do him no good if his opponent cheated. She felt hollow inside, wondering if they would ever be together like this again.

As she met Arthur's eyes, she knew he was thinking the same thing. But he would never say it. All he said was, "See you at the feast," and then he headed off to meet Valiant.

Merlin's eyes were closed. He was muttering the spell under his breath continually, but no longer had the energy to keep his eyelids open as well. His ears kept track of the passage of time, though – from the sounds of a crowing cockerel heralding the dawn to the distant cheers as Arthur and Valiant's fight began.

The young warlock couldn't help feeling that he should be there, lending his support to Arthur, but only his magic could help the prince, and he had to keep trying. There was a faraway roar from the crowd – and then, to his surprise, a growl much closer.

Much, much closer.

Merlin opened his eyes. A dog looked back at him.

He'd done it! He'd actually done it! He'd brought to life this huge, fierce, hungry-looking dog!

Ahh!

A few moments later, Gaius was surprised to see Merlin pelting down the corridor at top speed. "I'm on my way to the arena!" the boy gasped in passing. "And whatever you do – don't go into my room!"

CHAPTER EIGHTEEN
THE FINAL FIGHT

The arena had seen many battles, but none quite like this. Arthur and Valiant were both born warriors, and at least one of them knew he was fighting for his life. The blows they traded were fast and fierce. Gasps and shrieks as much as cheers and applause came from the watching crowd.

A skilful stroke from Arthur knocked off Valiant's helmet. The knight, stunned, staggered back – but Arthur didn't take advantage of the moment; he stepped back and removed his own helmet. The crowd applauded but Morgana cursed the prince for his chivalry.

A recovered Valiant showed no such gallantry. He charged at the prince, knocking him backwards.

Merlin arrived just in time to see Arthur's sword drop to the ground as Valiant pushed his opponent into the side of the arena. He stared in horror – without his helmet, Arthur's neck was exposed: the snakes would face no barrier . . .

But Arthur, knowing that death was upon him, lashed out with all his strength – and Valiant stumbled backwards, in full view of the crowd.

Frantically Merlin began the incantation. Valiant prepared to attack the unarmed prince once again – but a huge gasp suddenly came from the spectators. Two snakes were slithering from his shield!

"What are you doing? I didn't summon you!" he cried in fury – and fear.

"Guards, seize him!" Uther's men were on their way – but they weren't going to make it in time for Arthur.

"Now they can all see you for what you really are!" shouted Arthur.

But Valiant wasn't about to go quietly. "I might not be going to the feast now – but neither will you!" he cried. He looked down at the snakes. "Kill him!"

The snakes darted towards the unarmed prince.

The watching ladies screamed – all except Morgana. She might be a lady, but she had the heart of a warrior – and she was not going to let this

I MIGHT NOT BE GOING TO THE FEAST, BUT NEITHER ARE YOU. KILL HIM!

happen. She grabbed a sword from the scabbard of a nobleman in front of her, raised it in the air, threw . . . and the prince dived for the blade, caught it, swung it expertly . . .

The two snakes died instantly, their heads neatly sliced from their bodies. Then Valiant gasped in disbelief as the sword pierced his chest.

"Looks like I'll be going to the feast after all," Arthur whispered as the lifeless knight slipped to the ground.

The crowd cheered.

"My honourable guests, I give you Prince Arthur – your champion!"

The court applauded as Uther made the announcement. Arthur walked into the banqueting hall, arm in arm with Morgana, and nodded graciously to the crowd.

"Has your father apologized yet for not believing you?" Morgana whispered as they made their way down between the tables.

Arthur shrugged. "He'll never apologize." Then he smiled slightly. "I hope you're not disappointed that Valiant's not escorting you . . . ?"

"Turns out he wasn't really champion material." She smiled. "Actually, it's not every day a girl gets to save a prince."

"I wouldn't say I exactly needed saving," he protested. "I'm sure I would've thought of something . . ."

Morgana looked at him in disbelief. "So you're too proud to admit that you were saved by a girl?"

"Because I wasn't!"

"You know what, I wish Valiant *was* escorting me."

"Me too – then I wouldn't have to listen to you."

"Fine." Morgana pulled her arm away from Arthur and they glared at each other. Normal service had been resumed.

Merlin was surprised to see Arthur leave Morgana and head his way – but he was pleased too. Perhaps somehow Arthur had worked out that it was Merlin who had saved him!

His hopes were soon dashed. "Can you believe Morgana? She says she saved me. Like I needed any help."

Merlin sighed inwardly. If only Arthur knew!

The prince's next words were a more pleasant surprise, though. "I wanted to say: I made a mistake. It was unfair to sack you."

Merlin smiled, pleased. He'd seen enough of Camelot to know that it was a rare thing for royalty to apologize. "Don't worry about it. Buy me a drink. We'll call it even."

"I can't really be seen to be buying drinks for my servant . . ." Arthur protested.

"Your servant? You sacked me!"

"And now I'm re-hiring you. My chambers are a complete mess. My clothes need washing, my armour needs repairing, my boots need cleaning, my dogs need exercising, my fireplace needs sweeping, my bed needs changing, and someone needs to muck out my stables . . ."

Merlin listened in horror to the list of chores. But he wasn't really unhappy.

He could see that Arthur was brave and fearless and a great warrior – like his father. But unlike his father, he could admit to his mistakes. Who knew, perhaps he really would be a great king after all.

And somewhere deep inside, Merlin now knew that the Dragon's words were true – he belonged at Arthur's side. He would help the prince achieve great things.

It might not always be fun – but it would be worth it.

ALSO AVAILABLE

POTIONS AND POISON

Text by
Jacqueline Rayner

Based on the stories by Julian Jones
and Ben Vanstone

Continue the adventures at
bbc.co.uk/**merlin**

CHAPTER ONE
THE EGG

The ancient cave was dark and eerie, the stuff of nightmares. The woman who now stood within it, however, was young and beautiful – or at least, that was how she appeared. Her name was Nimueh and she was a sorceress, and it was magic that gave her both youth and beauty.

Magic was forbidden in King Uther's realms, on pain of death. Like many sorcerers, Nimueh hated the king, but unlike most of them she did not fear him.

Instead, she planned that one day he would fear *her*. And that day might just be today . . .

Nimueh picked up a handful of clay and began to mould it into the shape of a small, hunched creature. When it was finished to her satisfaction, she carefully placed the model in a carved ivory and gold eggshell, muttering incantations all the while.

She stroked the egg, and her

voice rose as the spell grew in power. This was magic of a kind few could master.

Beneath her fingers, the ivory became a sealed eggshell. It was still decorated with Nimueh's mark: four intersecting lines enclosing a single dot. From within the shell came a glow, outlining the silhouette of the clay model. And then there was something else – a light from the centre of the sculpture itself.

A glowing, beating heart.

The creature was alive.

In the middle of the cave was a carved column topped with a water-filled

stone basin. This was Nimueh's scrying bowl, through which she could observe the whole kingdom. Now she cast a further spell, creating a physical link with the world outside her cave, a passage between the bowl and the underground rivers that ran nearby. She tossed the egg into the basin and watched as the waters swirled it away. Her magic would make sure it went in the right direction. With a wave of her hand, the surface smoothed again, forming a picture of the egg's progress as it washed through underground rivers and streams until at last it surfaced in a pool – a pool beneath the citadel of Camelot.

Nimueh watched with glee as a tiny talon burst through the eggshell.

Oh yes, Uther would fear her now . . .